Fashionable Disaster

Read More
Trillium Sisters
Stories!

Trillium Sisters

Fashionable Disaster

Laura Brown and Elly Kramer

PIXEL✛INK

PIXEL✛INK

Text copyright © 2022 by Laura Brown and Elly Kramer

Interior Illustrations copyright © 2021 by TGM Development Corp.

All rights reserved

Pixel+Ink is a division of TGM Development Corp.

Printed and bound in November 2021 at Maple Press, York, PA, U.S.A.

Book design by Yaffa Jaskoll

www.pixelandinkbooks.com

Library of Congress Catalog-in-Publication: 2021930051

Hardcover ISBN 978-1-64595-064-6

Paperback ISBN 978-1-64595-065-3

eBook ISBN 978-1-64595-103-2

First Edition

1 3 5 7 9 10 8 6 4 2

This book, written during the Covid-19 pandemic, is for all the helpers who sustain our communities. Forever grateful.

—L.B. and E.K.

And for Reu. Thank you for all the magic you brought into my life.

—E.K.

CHAPTER 1

Giselle, Clare, Emmy, and Zee looked at one another and smiled.

"Ready," cried Giselle.

"Set," added Clare.

"Go!" Zee shouted.

Emmy giggled. "Last one to the tree house is a wilted flower!"

The kids took off on the narrow path through the woods, hopping over stones and tree roots.

When Giselle, who was in the lead, ducked to avoid a low-hanging branch, Zee zipped past her. "Hey, little man! How'd you get so fast?"

"I learned from the best."

"*Rrr, rrr, rrr,*" barked Fluffy. The wolf pup wiggled in the carrier strapped to Clare's back.

"I'm running as fast as I can," Clare insisted.

"Not fast enough," Zee teased, shooting ahead.

"Well, at least you're not in last place," said Emmy. She raced after her siblings, but only seemed to get farther behind. Finally, she threw her arms up in the air. "Just. Need. To. catch. My breath."

Clare looked over her shoulder. "Hold up, everyone. Let's wait for Emmy."

Giselle and Zee jogged back. "No worries,"

said Giselle. "We're farther from home than I realized. This is one long race!"

"Yep. It sure is," said Emmy. "Which means, I've got time to beat you!" With that, she took off again.

"Em, that's tricky," Zee called as he chased after her. "You weren't really out of breath."

"Right. It was the only way I could think to beat Giselle."

"Wrong!" Giselle cried as she whizzed past Emmy. "There's *no* way to beat me."

The kids raced into an even thicker part of the forest, dodging to avoid branches and bushes.

"I really do give up this time," Emmy called. She dropped to her knees, and in one easy motion, lifted Claw, her pet bear cub, from the sling she wore across her body.

"Me too," said Clare. "Who are we kidding? Nobody is faster than Giselle."

Emmy reached into her pocket and pulled out some granola. "Minis, snack time!" *Mini'mals* was the name the girls had given their pets. The sisters often called them *minis* for short.

Snack was all Soar, Giselle's pet eaglet, needed to hear. She flew off Giselle's shoulder and joined Claw and Fluffy, who were already licking up the treats.

"Em, I'm hungry, too," Zee complained. "Have you got any people snacks?"

"Sure." She pulled out an apple butter sandwich and handed everyone a piece. "But we can't stay too long. Dad needs my help at the Paw Pad this afternoon."

The Paw Pad was the animal clinic where their father, Dr. J.A., took care of the sick or injured animals living on Trillium Mountain. Whether it was an elk with a sore leg or a squirrel with teeth that needed trimming, Dr. J.A. made sure the animals stayed healthy. Emmy had just started to volunteer at the clinic. She loved helping the animals and spending time with her dad.

The kids finished their snack and were about to head home when they heard a splash.

"What was that?" Giselle asked.

"It sounded like water," said Emmy.

Clare wrinkled her nose. "In the middle of the forest? We're not near the river."

"The mini'mals are already investigating," Zee observed. "Come on."

Fluffy put his snout to the ground and nosed the underbrush. Claw and Soar were just behind. The kids hurried after their pets.

"How do the minis know where to go?" Zee asked. "We're off the trail now."

"Animals have better hearing and a stronger sense of smell than people," Emmy explained. "They may sense something that we can't."

"I hope you're right," said Clare. "I don't want to crawl through bushes for nothing."

Suddenly, the mini'mals stopped short. "*Yip, yip!*" went Soar. She beat her wings and flew up in the air.

"They found something!" Giselle said.

"Whoa!" Zee tipped his head back. In front of them was a sheet of rock that rose out of the ground. It continued up as high as the

evergreen trees and stretched as far as they could see in either direction. "What *is* this?"

"I don't know, buddy," Emmy said. "I thought we'd seen every part of Trillium Mountain, but I've never been here before."

Giselle held out her hand. "Zee, come with me. Em and Clare, you go the other way. Let's see just how far the rock goes."

"An adventure," Clare replied. "Love it!"

Zee, Giselle, and Soar headed right, while Clare, Emmy, Fluffy, and Claw went left.

"See anything besides rock?" Giselle called.

"Not yet!" shouted Clare. "It just keeps going and going."

"Then we'll keep going and going, too," Emmy declared.

Finally, Clare came to a spot where there

was a break in the rock. It was opposite where the land sloped up, becoming a hill.

"*Ahoo!*" Claw howled. She stood up on her hind legs and pawed at the opening.

"It's a way in, you guys!" Clare shouted.

"We're right behind you," Giselle called.

"Give me your hand, Clare," said Emmy. "I'll steady you if there's any problem."

Holding tight to her sister, Clare squeezed through the opening. Emmy followed her.

"Giselle, Zee, this is amazing!" Emmy cried. "Come look."

Inside, they gazed around, awed by what they'd found. The rock formed an area like a cave, but the top was open, letting the sunlight shine in. To one side was a dazzling pool, and on the other was flat ground with wild grass, flowers, and small trees.

Emmy thought it looked like the perfect place to lounge with a book.

"It's so beautiful," Clare said. "Let's stay here forever."

"That water is pretty inviting," Giselle added.

Zee looked around. "But what made the splash sound?"

They knelt by the pool, searching for clues.

"There! I think I found our noise maker." Emmy pointed to some fish, which were similar in color to the bottom of the pool and hard to spot.

Zee giggled. "Those fish are cool, but they aren't making any noise."

But then, *Splash!*

"*Rrr, rrr, rrr!*" barked Fluffy. He raced along the edge of the pool.

"Jumping junipers!" Giselle cried. "Look at the fish leap!"

"I guess fish *do* make noise," said Clare.

Zee ran to the pool's edge. "I want to swim with the fishies." He pulled off his sneakers, but Emmy held up a hand.

"Hold on. Let's make sure it's safe." She walked around the pool. "No big rocks and not too deep. That's good." She dipped a fingertip into the water. "Ooo, and it's warm!"

"So, can I go in now?" Zee begged.

"We don't have swimsuits," Emmy noted.

"But it's warm out and the water's not that deep. We'll be okay," Giselle said.

That was all Zee needed to hear. He splashed in. The minis followed him. "*Yip, Ahoo, Rrrr!*" Fluffy plunged her head underwater trying to catch a fish, but they were too fast.

"I'm going in," Giselle announced.

"G, wait! You don't want your shirt to get soaked." Clare grabbed the hem and tied the bottom in a side knot.

"Thanks," said Giselle. "Smart and stylish."

"Yeah, that does look super cool," Emmy agreed.

"Here, Em." Clare took a bandana and swept Emmy's hair into a high ponytail. "I know you hate getting your hair wet."

Emmy swung her head back and forth. "You know me too well, sis. I love it!"

Then Giselle and Emmy waded in.

"Wow, this water *is* warm," said Giselle. "Yum."

"How's that possible?" Clare wondered.

"This could be a warm spring," Emmy replied. "Heat from deep in the earth makes the water warm."

Giselle sank a little deeper. "Well, whatever it is, it feels great. Aren't you coming in, Clare?"

"Just wondering if I should take my trillium petal charm earring off first."

Giselle and Emmy looked down at their

own jewelry. Giselle's blue charm, which she wore as an anklet, was already wet. It sparkled beneath the water. "Mine's fine."

"Well, in that case," said Clare, "watch out!" She stepped in and started splashing.

Zee shook the water from his face, then grinned. "Natural spring water fight!"

CHAPTER 2

The kids climbed out of the pool to dry off in the late morning sun. Everyone felt happy and warm.

Giselle giggled. "So much for keeping our clothes dry."

"Yep," agreed Emmy. "I've gotta change. Can't show up to the Paw Pad like this."

"And you promised to practice soccer kicks with me, Gelly," said Zee.

Giselle squeezed her brother to her side.

"One hundred percent. But I'm happy we found this place. It feels like we've discovered a hidden treasure."

"Yeah." Emmy nodded. "Like our own secret clubhouse."

"Don't ya think, Clare?" Giselle asked. The girls looked at their sister, but she seemed lost in her own thoughts.

Emmy moved closer to Clare. "You okay, sis? You haven't said a word since we got out of the spring."

"I'm fine. Just thinking," Clare answered softly.

"Think all you want," said Giselle. "We'll get Zee and the minis ready to go home." She bent to tie Zee's sneakers when suddenly water sprayed onto their faces.

"Fluffy!" said Giselle. The wolf pup was shaking the water off of his fur.

Clare wiped her cheek and turned back to the water. She loved her sisters with all of her heart. Nobody was as passionate as Giselle or as kind as Emmy. But lately, Clare had been feeling a little sad. Her sisters had their own ways of helping. Giselle taught Zee about sports. And Emmy helped at the clinic. Clare frowned. *I want to help, too, but how?*

Emmy gave Clare's shoulder a squeeze. "I love this ponytail." She wagged her head back and forth so her hair swung from side to side.

"I'm keeping my hair like this all day!"

"And I'm wearing my shirt Clare-style for soccer," Giselle added. "It doesn't get in my way like this!"

Clare smiled. *I made them both feel good.*

She sat up straighter. What if she could find a way to share this natural spring with the rest of Trillville? It was too fun and pretty to keep a secret. The warm water might make people feel good, just like the fashion tricks she'd shared with her sisters had. "That's it!"

"*What's* it?" asked Giselle.

"I've got an idea, and it involves you, Emmy, and this gorgeous spring!"

"Well, don't just sit there," Emmy insisted.

"Yeah," Giselle added. "Spill!"

CHAPTER 3

Clare threw her arms wide. "This place is so fantastic, we've got to share it with others."

"Clare," Emmy began, "that is so—"

"Trillsome!" Giselle finished.

The mini'mals seemed to agree. They wagged their backsides, and Soar flapped her wings.

"But what exactly should we do?" asked Emmy.

"Maybe we could bring people here on tours?" Giselle suggested.

"Or turn the spring into a swimming pool?" Emmy mused. "Everyone can float and splash, just like we did."

Clare was happy that her sisters liked her idea, but that wasn't exactly what she had in mind. "I was kinda thinking . . . both."

"Both?" Emmy scratched her head. "Now you really have to spill!"

"What if we did something bigger?" Clare continued. She paused.

The wait was too much for Zee. "What? What are we going to do?"

"What if we made this warm spring a spa, so everyone on the mountain can enjoy it!"

Fluffy raced around her, wagging his tail.

"That's a cool idea," Emmy began, "but we'd need lots of supplies. Towels and chairs."

"Face masks? Nail polish?" Giselle added. "How would we pay for all that?"

"Well, I've been thinking about that," Clare responded quickly. Her sisters weren't surprised. Clare was an idea girl. "What if the spa were a business? We'd charge people a little, and we'd use the money to buy supplies."

"Dancing daisies, that could work!" cried Giselle.

Clare clapped her hands together. "And here's the best part. I've got a name. We could call it . . . the Soak and Spring."

"Or how about the *Sisters'* Soak and Spring?" Emmy suggested.

"Yes, that's even better," Clare agreed.

"*Ahoo!*" Fluffy and Claw howled.

"*Yip, yip, yip!*" Soar added, flapping her wings so hard, she rose off the ground.

"I'm excited," said Clare. "Trillizens can come to the spa to soak in the warm spring, drink some daisy juice, and get treatments. That way, they'll feel good, even after they've left."

"Treatments? You mean like cucumbers on your eyes?" Emmy asked. "I love those!"

"You betcha," Clare replied. "We'll have manicures, too."

Claw tapped her paws on the ground.

"I think Claw wants a *pawdicure*," Zee observed.

"Why not?" Clare grinned. "Everyone gets to feel good here."

"And can we have warm towels that smell

like flowers?" Giselle asked.

"For sure!" said Clare. "And, if we have money left after we buy all the supplies, we'll donate it to Dad's clinic."

Huge smiles broke out on Emmy's and Giselle's faces.

"Clare, your spa is a totally trillsome idea," said Emmy. "Congrats."

"Yep. Cool, creative, and very Clare," added Giselle.

Clare smiled wide. Maybe she had found her own way of helping.

CHAPTER 4

Emmy jumped to her feet and held out the bear wrap for Claw. The little cub settled in, wrapping her arms and legs around Emmy's waist. "Trills, this is super exciting, but I promised Dad I'd help him this afternoon. It's almost lunchtime. I've got to get home."

"Sure," said Clare. "I just want to jot down what we'll need for the spa so I don't forget." She pulled a little pad out of her backpack and started a list. "Gosh, there's so much to do!" She rubbed her pink earring charm. "I wish we could use our magic to help us."

Giselle laughed. "Our magic would only activate if relaxing at a spa was an emergency!"

Emmy turned to Clare. "Sis, question: I know we're going to use the money we make to buy supplies, but how are we going to pay for the supplies we need for the first day? Towels, nail polish, and refreshments aren't cheap."

"Hmmm. I didn't think of that," said Clare.

Pet sitting? Parent sitting? Sister sitting? Each idea was sillier than the last.

But Clare wasn't laughing. She needed another awesome way to make money for the first-day supplies.

Giselle put an arm around her sister. "Don't worry, you'll think of something, Clare. You always do." Then she whistled for Soar. The little bird hopped into her arms and Giselle settled her on her shoulder.

Suddenly, Clare smiled brightly. "Got it!"

"Great. Tell us!" Zee demanded. When everyone looked in his direction, he shrugged. "What? I love her ideas, too."

"We'll have a fashion show!" Clare exclaimed.

Zee looked confused. "How does that solve the problem?"

"People will buy tickets to come to the fashion show. We'll use that money for the opening-day supplies at the spa," explained Clare.

Giselle opened her mouth to ask a question, but Clare held up a hand. She was on a roll. "Plus, we won't spend a cent on the show itself. We'll *borrow* the clothes from stores in town."

Giselle thought for a moment, then slowly started nodding. "That could work."

"It sounds fun," Emmy agreed. She strutted by the pool, pretending to be a model. "Check me out!"

Giselle twirled in place. "Look at me, dahhhling."

"We'll stage the show right next to the pool, so everyone gets a sneak peek of the spa setup. That way, people will be excited about the spa before it even opens!"

Giselle was glad to see her sister so happy. "Sounds perf—"

"Dancing daisies," Clare interrupted. "Why should people just *watch* the fashion show?"

"Because it's a show?" Zee replied.

"True. But our neighbors can be *part* of the show. How fun would it be to see Mayor Mae as a model?"

"The funnest!" Zee shouted, bouncing up and down.

"I love the idea of everyone in Trillville working together," Giselle added.

Clare hugged herself. She was so excited.

The kids made sure the minis were safe and then walked toward the opening in the rock wall. But just as they were about to exit, they heard a rumbling noise. Giselle pulled Zee back just in time.

Boom! It sounded like something had hit the other side of the rock wall, not far from where they were standing.

"What was that?" asked Clare.

Giselle poked her head out of the opening. "I think something rolled down that hill and smacked into the wall."

"Let's go see," said Emmy.

One by one, the kids made their way through the gap in the wall.

"Look!" said Zee. "It's almost as big as me."

A small boulder sat against the rock face, not far from the opening. It looked like pieces had splintered off and were scattered all around it.

Emmy looked up at the hill. "There are other big rocks up there. What if another one rolls down?"

"What are the chances of that happening twice?" Clare asked.

Giselle shrugged. "Probably slim to none."

"See? There's nothing to worry about," Clare insisted. Her spa idea was too good to be bowled over by a runaway rock.

"I guess," said Emmy reluctantly, touching the green charm that hung over her heart. Still, she couldn't help glancing up the hill as they headed home.

CHAPTER 5

Back at the tree house, the girls had lunch, then raced up the ladder to their room. Clare dove onto her hammock and started adding to her to-do list.

Dr. J.A. popped his head into the doorway. "Helloooo, my sunshines! Did you have fun in the forest?"

The sisters all started speaking at once.

"Whoa, whoa, whoa," Dr. J.A. said, laughing. "One at a time so I can hear you.

You found a hidden natural spring?"

"You know it! The water was incredibly warm. It felt yummy," replied Giselle.

"And I checked that the water was flowing through dirt and rocks, like you taught me," added Emmy.

"Yup. That's a good clue that the water is fresh and clean," agreed their father. "Now, let me get this straight. You want to make it into a spa for the Trillizens?"

"We can't wait," said Clare. She explained their fashion show plan to raise money.

"Well, that sounds fashiontastic!" Dr. J.A. slipped off a shoe and wiggled his toes. "Look at my poor feet. They could use the Sisters' Soak and Spring, don't ya think?"

Giselle pinched her nose. "P.U., Dad. Your

feet definitely need the Soak and Spring, and maybe a little soap."

"Then I'll be sure to make an appointment." He paused in the doorway. "Em, I've got some paperwork to do. Let's leave for the Paw Pad in an hour or so."

Clare turned to her sisters. "Great! We can work on the show until you have to leave."

"But I'm supposed to run soccer drills with Zee," Giselle reminded Clare.

"He's playing upstairs. He can wait a little, can't he?"

"I guess," replied Giselle.

"Speaking of the fashion show," Emmy began, "are you sure another rock won't roll down the hill? If people are waiting to get into the show, they could get hit."

"Em," Claire replied. "What are the chances of that happening?"

Emmy blushed. It didn't seem likely.

"Now, I have some great ideas to make the spring comfy for the audience. I was thinking we'd use our extra blankets for people to sit on while they watch the show."

Emmy brightened. "Ooo, that does sound comfy! We have some cuddly ones in the closet downstairs. I'll go get them."

Clare smiled. *This can work. I just have to get Emmy excited, and then she'll forget about those silly rocks.*

"Perfect, thank you. Let's see. What's next? The water needs to be skimmed, and we'll need snacks. I'm thinking jelly beans. We'll line them up by color. And we'll have daisy juice with the cutest umbrellas in the cups."

"Whoa, Clare," Giselle said. "You've thought of everything! But wouldn't it be easier to mix the jelly beans? They'd look so pretty that way, like a rainbow."

"Hmm. I don't know, G," Clare answered. "Mixing may look messy."

Giselle lifted an eyebrow. Clare usually loved her ideas.

Meanwhile, Emmy returned with the blankets and started to assemble a basket of nail polish to bring to the spa.

"Hey, Em, let's do that *after* the fashion

show. And please, sort the polish by color, just like the jelly beans. Like I told Giselle, I'm not really feeling rainbows these days."

Emmy put the basket down and looked at Clare. This wasn't like her sister. She usually listened to everyone.

But Clare didn't notice. "Oh, and we have to get the word out! We'll need invitations and flyers to hang around town."

"Great," began Giselle. "I have some ideas—"

"That's okay," Clare interrupted. "I already have a perfect idea for the invitations. Please, just do your job on the list. That's why I made it."

Giselle stood gaping at her sister like one of the fish in the spring.

"Hold on. Who put you in charge?" blurted out Emmy.

Clare looked up from her list, then shrugged. "Well, I guess I did. I came up with the idea for the spa and the show."

Emmy and Giselle exchanged a look. It was true. They *had been* Clare's ideas. But the

sisters didn't usually worry about *who* came up with an idea. They were more of a team than that.

Giselle drew in a deep breath. *I want this day to be perfect for Clare. She's so excited.* She slowly exhaled. "Fine. We'll follow your list."

"Yeah," agreed Emmy. "After all, this is about helping the community. We're all for that."

CHAPTER 6

Clare was so excited about the fashion show, she woke up early the next morning. Her sisters were still sound asleep in their hammocks, while the mini'mals snored softly on the floor. Clare tiptoed into the craft room next to their bedroom and got to work.

A few hours later, Emmy and Giselle sleepily shuffled in.

"Look who's finally up," said Clare.

"Finally? It's only eight thirty." Giselle stretched, then took in the magazines, scissors, glue, and scraps of paper scattered all over the floor. "What *is* all this?"

"It looks like an idea explosion in here," Emmy added.

Clare picked up a poster that showed dresses, necklaces, earrings, shoes, and hats in various shades of blue. "I guess I did get up a little early," she admitted. "I had so many ides in my head, I couldn't sleep. What do you think about using outfits like these for the fashion show?"

"Beautiful," said Emmy. "I never would have thought to put all that together."

"Yeah, they really pop," Giselle agreed.

"Thanks, guys. I also designed flyers for us

to hand out today." Clare looked around sheepishly. "Maybe I went a little overboard."

"I haven't even brushed my teeth yet. I feel like such a slacker!" Giselle joked.

"Well, the early bird gets the worm—or the coolest outfit." Clare giggled. "Seriously, as soon as you're both dressed, please call the shop owners in town and ask if we can borrow clothes like these for the show. We've gotta move!"

"Don't worry, sis," said Emmy. "That sounds pretty doable."

"Yeah, but it's only the first thing to do. After you make the calls, please run into town and pick up the clothes. Then go to the hardware store and borrow a pool skimmer. Next, hit the grocery store for the jelly beans and ingredients for daisy juice. We'll use the money in my bear bank for the food and pay me back later. Here." Clare turned her bank upside down, and coins poured out into Emmy's hands. "Hmmm. I think I'm forgetting something."

"Clare, that's a lot! And it sounds like you've given us *all* the jobs. What are *you* doing?" Giselle demanded.

"Me?" Clare paused for a minute to think. "I'm doing the most important job of all. Getting the word out! No customers, no spa!"

"Okaaay. You don't have to get snippy." Giselle rolled her eyes. She would have preferred to choose her own job, but this was Clare's big idea. If her sister wanted her to make calls and pick up clothes, she would do it.

"I can't wait to see the clothes," said Emmy, trying to sound enthusiastic.

"Me either," Clare replied. "You two better get going. We need everything here by lunch."

Emmy rubbed her ears. Maybe she hadn't heard correctly. "Did you say lunch?"

"Of course. The show's tomorrow night. Once everything's here, we have to bring it to the spring," Clare explained as she handed the list to Emmy.

Giselle blinked. "That's really fast. What if we can't get everything done in time?"

"Not an option, G. We *have* to!" Clare pointed at her watch. "I'm gonna head to Trillville to let people know about the show. I'll meet up with you later." Clare grabbed her jacket and the flyers and started toward the door, but her sisters weren't moving. *What are they waiting for? There is so much that needs to get done!* "C'mon, Trills, move it!" she growled before heading out.

Sighing, Giselle and Emmy started to get ready. Giselle scrubbed her teeth really hard.

"You okay?" asked Emmy.

"Is it just me or is Clare being bossy? Who does she think she is ordering us around?"

"She isn't acting like herself," Emmy agreed. "It's annoying. But there *is* a lot to do. Maybe she'll calm down once we have all the stuff?"

"Maybe," Giselle replied, wiping her face. "I guess we'll have to wait and see."

CHAPTER 7

"Thanks for lending us the hat, Mrs. Lilienstern. We can't wait to see you, either!" Giselle hung up the phone. "Well, that was the last call. We got everything on this list."

"*Phew!* So, we have the hat, dresses, and jewelry?" Emmy asked.

"Uh-huh. Plus, the shoes. I guess we should go pick everything up," said Giselle, but she didn't sound happy.

"Yup," Emmy answered glumly. "I hope once Clare hears all the progress we've made, she'll be nicer."

Giselle touched the charm around her ankle as she put her on shoes. Emmy played with her own charm hanging over her heart. "I miss the three of us working together," Giselle said.

"So do I. We Trills are awesome together. When our charms activate, we're unstoppable. But with Clare bossing us around, it doesn't feel like we're a team."

"I know. We never would have been able to save the bees without all of our suggestions."

"Abso-trilly," Emmy agreed. "If there was an emergency right now, I bet Clare wouldn't listen to us. And then what?"

Soar nuzzled up against Giselle, and Claw plopped down next to Emmy. Somehow, the minis seemed to know the sisters needed some love. "Aww, thanks, Soar," said Giselle as she stroked her feathers.

Emmy buried her face in Claw's soft fur. When she sat up, she felt more hopeful. "There's no stronger bond than sisters. We'll find a way to make Clare listen. We have to."

CHAPTER 8

Emmy and Giselle arrived at Mrs. Lilienstern's boutique, Hats and Cats. It was where Clare bought all of her cat headbands.

"Oh, hi, guys," Clare said when her sisters walked in.

"What are you doing here?" Emmy asked.

"Yeah, we thought you were out advertising," added Giselle. "That was *your* very important job, remember?"

"Totally," Clare said quickly. "I just . . . well, you see . . . everything has to be exactly right for the fashion show. I wanted to make sure the hat looked perfect."

"Clare, we can make sure it's perfect just as well as you can," growled Giselle.

Just then, Mrs. Lilienstern brought out the hat. It was a work of art, woven from feathers in various shades of blue. Each feather had been found on the forest floor, washed, and then dyed before being added to the design. Mrs. Lilienstern laid a pair of blue feather earrings on the counter beside the hat. Her eyes sparkled. "I couldn't resist. I thought they would go perfectly together."

"They do! Thank you so much for—"

Clare stopped as her eyes caught something in the display case.

Mrs. Lilienstern followed her gaze. "You've always had a *purr*fect eye when it comes to cat headbands, Clare," she said, pulling out a few blue bejeweled pieces.

"These are so beautiful!" Clare clapped her in hands in delight.

"Then they're yours for the show." Mrs. Lilienstern smiled as she handed Clare a bag.

"Ahem." Emmy looked pointedly at Clare, then turned her gaze toward Mrs. Lilienstern.

"Oh, yes! Mrs. Lilienstern, we'd love it if you were one of the models in the show."

"I'm honored," said Mrs. Lilienstern.

"Is that a yes?" asked Giselle.

"It sure is. I can't wait. But promise me

that the first spa appointment is mine. My nails are a mess!"

"You got it," Clare said enthusiastically.

Back on the street, Clare started handing out flyers. "Where should you go? To our fashion show!" After a few minutes, she whispered to her sisters, "You should get the rest of the items on the list."

"In a bit," Emmy replied. "I'm thirsty. We've been walking all over town. Let's grab some daisy juice before we get the pool skimmer."

"Great idea," said Giselle.

"No. There's no time—" Clare stopped mid-sentence to hand a Trillizen a flyer. "See you tonight," she said and waved. Then she turned back to Giselle and Emmy. "Oh, I forgot to put little umbrellas on the list! Can you pick those up, too?"

"We're thirsty," Emmy protested.

Clare rolled her eyes, then rummaged in her pockets and pulled out a granola bar. "Here. This should help."

"A granola bar?" Giselle said. "We're thirsty, not hungry!"

"The bar's fine. Have a nibble and keep going," Clare insisted. "I've got to advertise!"

Just then, Mayor Mae called, "Hi, Trills. Perfect timing. I was going to leave the necklace you asked to borrow at the Paw Pad, but since you're here . . ." She sat on a nearby bench, removed a jewelry box from her bag, and opened it to reveal a pendant made from a geode. The stone was a stunning aqua color,

the exact same shade as the water in the warm spring. "This beauty was found right here on Trillium Mountain. It's been in my family for generations."

"It's magnificent," Emmy whispered.

"And perfect for a fashion show that benefits the whole mountain," agreed Giselle.

"That's why I wanted to help," said Mayor Mae. "The whole town is excited about the show, and everyone is so touched by what you're doing for the community."

Clare removed the hat, earrings, and headbands from her bag and held the necklace next to them. The colors complemented one another beautifully. "Thank you so much, Mayor Mae. We have one more thing to ask of you. Will you walk in the show?"

"I'd love to," the mayor replied. She held up the geode and struck a pose. "How do I look?"

"Trilltastic!" Clare said.

Mayor Mae returned the necklace to the box and handed it to Clare. "Just be careful with the borrowed items."

Emmy opened her mouth, but Clare yanked her arm.

"We'll be beyond careful," Clare assured her. "Thanks again, Mayor Mae. See you at the show!"

"Clare," said Emmy, "why'd you pull me away?"

"There's no time for chitchat! You can talk to Mayor Mae *after* the show."

Emmy glared at her sister, but Clare didn't

notice. She was already passing out more flyers. Giselle grabbed Emmy's hand and walked toward the grocery store. They needed to pick up the last items so they'd have time for lunch before the afternoon's work began.

CHAPTER 9

Emmy and Giselle struggled through the front door of the tree house with their shopping bags.

"Wowza! Did you borrow everything in town?" Dr. J.A. asked as he rushed to help.

"Yep, we got everything on Clare's list," Emmy explained.

"It was hard work," added Giselle. "We're starving!"

"Lunch is almost ready. Time to wash up," said their dad.

The girls clambered up the ladder to their room. As Dr. J.A. stirred the pasta, he glanced in the bags. He lifted out a pair of turquoise suede men's loafers just as Clare arrived home.

"Dad! Don't peek!"

Dr. J.A. dropped the shoes back into the bag. "Okay, but those sure are blue-tiful. Tomorrow is going to be great."

"Thanks." Clare's eyes lingered on the loafers. "I was gonna ask you.

Have you ever thought about modeling?"

"Who, me? I thought you'd never ask!" He slipped his feet into the shoes and pretended to model them. Just then, Giselle, Emmy, and Zee raced down the ladder into the kitchen.

"Is the pasta ready?" asked Zee.

"Yep," Dad replied. "You three look comfy. Grab a bowl."

Giselle, Emmy, and Zee sat at the table, but Clare stood staring at her siblings, arms crossed. "What are you guys wearing?" she asked, like she was accusing them of a crime.

"We put on sweats and slippers," Emmy replied.

"This morning was a workout," Giselle added. "We're relaxing a little before we help more."

"There isn't time to relax! The show is tomorrow. We have to get everything to the spring or we'll never be ready!" Clare grabbed the bags of clothes and stormed up the ladder.

Angry tears stung her eyes as she threw herself on her hammock. *Don't Giselle and Emmy know how important this show is to me?*

"*Ahoo.*"

Clare turned to see Fluffy looking at her, curious. She smiled as he leapt onto the hammock and licked her face.

"Thanks, Fluff. I needed that." At least her pup was still with her. She popped one of the headbands on him. "Who's a handsome boy?"

Fluffy wagged his tail.

"Knock, knock. Can I come in?" Dr. J.A. stood at the doorway with a bowl of pasta.

"Sure," said Clare.

"That was a pretty quick exit, honey. What's going on?"

"I'm mad at Giselle and Emmy. They'd rather rest than help with my show."

"*Your* show?" Dr. J.A. asked with one eyebrow raised.

"I mean, *our* show. But it was my idea."

"They're tired after such a busy morning. Sounds like you all worked really hard."

"Sure. But there's still so much to do."

"Honey, let's not forget they spent their whole morning helping you. Everyone works at a different pace."

Clare frowned. "I guess."

"Well, I *know*. Besides, I've seen the three of you do some pretty incredible things when you listen to one another and work together." He gave Clare's arm a squeeze.

Clare sighed. She knew her dad had a point, but all she could think about were supplies that needed to be transported to the spring. If her sisters kept taking breaks, she'd never be ready.

"Dad, would *you* help me bring the supplies to the spring this afternoon?"

"At your service," Dr. J.A. said. "Bring that bowl downstairs when you're done and we'll head out. In the meantime, I'm going to practice for the show." He gave her a wink as he left the room.

CHAPTER 10

Clare woke up the next morning and jumped out of bed. Even though her father had helped her set up the spa at the spring, there was still lots to do before the show. *Where are Emmy and Giselle? We have to get to the spring!* Clare threw on her clothes and slipped down the ladder.

"Surprise!" her sisters called as her feet hit the floor.

"Ahoo!" went Claw, wagging her bottom in excitement.

"Yip, yip," Soar tweeted.

"What's going on?" asked Clare.

Giselle led her sister to the head of the table and made her sit, then Emmy placed a smiley face made out of waffles and berries in front of her. "For you. Today's going to be great!"

Clare was quiet. She looked at the breakfast, then pushed the plate away. "Thanks, Trills, but I'm going to grab a bar on my way to the spring. No time to hang out."

"Clare, you can't be serious," said Giselle. "You're not even going to have a bite? We got up early to make this for you."

Clare shook her head.

"Is this about yesterday?" Emmy asked. "We said we were sorry."

"Girls, come on," said Dr. J.A. "You shook hands and made up at dinner last night."

"I know. It's not about yesterday. I just can't think about anything but the fashion

show right now." She looked down at her feet. "See? I even put on someone else's shoes."

"I thought those looked familiar," said Emmy with a small smile.

Dr. J.A. let out a soft chuckle and handed Clare her own shoes. "You have a lot on your mind, sweetheart."

"That's why I've gotta go! Trills, get to the spring as soon as you can. Tonight has to be perfect." With that, Clare ran out the door.

Dr. J.A. grabbed Clare's jacket and hurried into the yard after her.

When the door closed, Giselle dumped the breakfast into the trash and started to scrub the counter.

"Easy! It's not the counter's fault," Emmy said gently.

"It seems like Clare only cares about her beloved show," Giselle grumbled.

"I don't even want to go to the show anymore."

Giselle looked down at her charm. "I miss the three of us."

They slipped back into silence as they washed the dishes.

Finally, Giselle put away the last pan. "Sis, this fashion show has made Clare a real sour flower."

"Perfectly put." Emmy giggled.

"But sisters are forever."

Emmy hugged Giselle tightly. "You're right, G." She took a deep breath. They were sisters and the show had to go on.

CHAPTER 11

"Okay, game faces on," Giselle said as they arrived at the natural spring. Claw and Soar followed happily behind them.

Emmy put on the biggest grin she could muster. "I'm all smiles, see?"

But when they stepped inside the rocky enclosure, they didn't have to pretend. Dr. J.A. and Clare must have worked for hours because the transformation was incredible!

They had cleared a path along the curve of the pool for the models to walk down. The extra blankets lined the path, all soft blues, whites, and pinks. Clare had reused the clear cellophane from the jelly beans to make lanterns. Fireflies flitted in and out of the lanterns, illuminating the path. Fluffy was jumping on the blankets to give them extra fluff, wagging his tail happily. Clare stood by a flat rock she was using as a tabletop, laying out baby-blue paper cups and placing umbrellas in each.

"Clare, wow!" Emmy exclaimed.

"You and Dad did a lot of work yesterday," Giselle agreed. "Everything looks really nice."

Clare looked up. "Ah, thank goodness you're here."

Giselle opened her arms for a hug, but

Clare handed her the pool skimmer instead. "Fish out anything gross floating in the water."

Giselle raised an eyebrow.

"You know, like dead bugs or leaves. Clear?" Clare asked.

"Crystal."

Clare dropped some mini umbrellas into Emmy's hands. "Can you take over here? I'm going to check on Fluffy and the blankets. Everything has to be just—"

"Perfect. We know," Giselle said, but Clare was already walking away. Emmy got to work while Giselle skimmed leaves and feathers out of the spring.

"Em, no!" Clare called. "The umbrellas should be leaning against the right side of the glass!"

Emmy saluted. "Yes, ma'am!"

Giselle walked around the pool, looking for any last leaves. "This looks pretty good to me."

"Pretty good isn't good enough," Clare snapped. "Is that an *ant* in the water?"

Giselle stared at her sister. "Clare, we're in the middle of nature. We can't tell the bugs to leave! Besides, *you* chose this location. Wasn't the idea of being outdoors part of the charm?"

"But it looks sloppy!" Clare shot back. "If you can't do it right, then don't do it at all."

"Fine by me!" Giselle threw the skimmer in the air, watching it flatten one of Clare's perfectly fluffed blankets as it landed.

"Hopefully, *one* of my sisters can follow instructions," Clare grumbled, turning back to Emmy. But when she saw the cups, her face fell. "Em, I *told* you! All the umbrellas should lean against the right side of the glass."

"Really, Clare?" Emmy shouted. "You can't even say thank you? We're trying to help, but you've done nothing but boss everyone around the past two days."

"Yeah," Giselle chimed in. "We've listened to all of your ideas. You haven't asked what we thought even once."

"We're supposed to be a team, but you've made this all about you," Emmy complained.

"Ah, come on, Trills. I know we're a team. But the fashion show and the spa were my ideas, so I'm in charge."

"You know what? I don't really like you when you're in charge," Emmy said, dropping the rest of the umbrellas at Clare's feet.

"And we're sick of your stupid ideas," Giselle added.

"WE QUIT!" they shouted together.

"Fine!" Clare huffed. "If I do everything myself, at least it'll be done right."

"Good luck with that," Giselle yelled as she turned away.

Fluffy stood between the girls, whimpering. "Fluffy, you're with me!" Clare called. The pup trotted after her with his tail between his legs. Clare picked up the little wolf, hugging him close. "Who needs them? I'll show them how to put on a show."

CHAPTER 12

Giselle and Emmy scooped up their pets and stomped toward town.

"Wanna finally get that daisy juice, Em?" Giselle asked.

"On the triple!" Emmy replied. "Let's go."

Back at the spring, Clare laid the last program and stepped back to admire her work. The water sparkled. The blankets looked irresistible. *Dancing daisies, I've done a terrific job!*

She felt something splat on her nose and looked up. Rain! Clare's heart began to race. A soggy fashion show would be no fun. She had to do something. *You have good ideas. You can get yourself out of this.*

As it rained harder, the earth beside the pool turned muddy and began to run into the spring water. Clare almost cried as she watched the pool turn from a dazzling blue to an awful brownish green. She turned and saw that the blankets and programs were now soaked.

She looked for somewhere to avoid the rain. As she turned in circles searching for a dry nook, she heard a noise like a low rumble. It got louder and faster. Clare looked out through the opening in the wall and gasped. Just like the day they'd discovered the spring, rocks were sliding down the hill toward the wall! The mud must have loosened them. Stones as small as her fist were sliding into bigger rocks, piling up and pushing against them. Before Clare's eyes, a small boulder began to wobble from the pressure.

"*Rrrr, rrr, rrr!*" Fluffy barked.

"That's not gonna stop them," Clare said.

And then the boulder gave way, rolling down the hill.

"Rockslide!" Clare called out. They ran for cover. Clare hid her face in Fluffy's neck.

Whack! The ground shook under their feet. And then everything was eerily quiet. Even the rain had stopped.

Clare took a deep breath to calm her racing heart. "I think we're okay, Fluff. *Phew.*"

"*Ahoo.*" Fluffy whimpered.

"What's wrong, puppy?"

"*Ahoo.*" Fluffy trotted to the entrance.

Clare followed, sucking in a breath when she saw the problem. The boulder that had rolled down the hill now blocked the only opening to the natural spring!

"Uh-oh," Clare cried. "How are people going to get inside to watch the show? And"— she paused, realization dawning on her—"if people can't get *into* the show, how are *we* going to get *out*?"

Breathe. I always have good ideas. I'll come up with something.

"Aha!" Clare snapped her fingers as she scanned the rock around her. She crossed to the wall and tried to climb up it. "If I can just find some spots to hold on to, I may be able to get to the top. Then I'll see if there's a way to scale down the other side."

But the rain had made the rock wall very slick. "Sour flowers," she said as she crashed to the ground for the fifth time. She slumped down and cradled her head in her hands, trying not to panic. They were trapped. She should have listened to her sisters about the dangers of those falling rocks.

Her sisters! She needed them now more than ever.

"What are we going to do, Fluff?" she asked as she stroked the soft fur on his ears.

Suddenly, Fluffy ran over to a skinny tree that grew close to the rocky wall. He dug his nails into the trunk and pulled himself up the tree, bit by bit. The narrow trunk swayed from side to side, but held. When Fluffy got to the highest branch, he was only a few feet from the top of the wall.

Clare knew her brave pup was going to leap. "No, Fluff," she called. Fluffy sprang from the tree, caught the top edge of the wall with his front paws, then slid up and over. Clare watched as he disappeared down the other side.

"Fluffy!" Clare cried. "Are you okay?" There was silence. She shivered. After a

moment, she heard "*Rrr, rrr, rrr!*" from the other side. She ran and pressed her arms against the wall. "Good boy! Go get help."

"*Rrr, rrr, rrr!*" Fluffy barked.

Clare sank to the ground. All she could do was wait. Fluffy was her last hope.

CHAPTER 13

Giselle and Emmy walked quietly toward town. Soar rode on Giselle's shoulder and Claw sat comfortably in the bear wrap strung diagonally from Emmy's left shoulder to her right hip.

"I thought I'd feel calmer by now," Giselle said, "but I'm still pretty mad. Is it terrible that I don't want to go back and help Clare?"

"I feel the same way," replied Emmy. "I

know we *should* go back, but I just can't handle another lecture."

Suddenly, there was a rustling in the bushes behind them. Then they heard, "*Rrr, rrr, rrr.*" That sounded a lot like Fluffy. And suddenly there he was, running toward them. But he was limping.

Emmy dropped to her knees. "Fluff, what happened, boy?" She went to touch his front leg, and he whimpered in pain.

"Sorry, sweetie," she murmured. She wrapped her arms around him. But instead of calming down, Fluffy barked more. "This can't be good. Something must have happened to—"

"Clare!" interrupted Giselle. "We gotta go. Now!"

"But his leg, Giselle," said Emmy. "He's hurt."

"What if Clare's hurt, too?"

"Oh, I hope not." Emmy handed the pup to Giselle to carry while they ran.

Without another word, Giselle and Emmy raced back toward the spring. Their anger was gone. They only cared about reaching their sister as fast as possible.

CHAPTER 14

As they got closer to the spring, Emmy's green necklace charm lifted into the air and Giselle's blue anklet charm stretched away from her leg.

"G, do you feel your charm pulling?" Emmy asked.

"I was just about to ask you the same thing." Giselle looked down. "The charms only move like this in an emergency."

"I know! Which means—" Emmy's

sneaker slid, and she almost fell. "The charms are trying to combine," she said as she steadied herself.

"The ground here is really wet," Giselle noted. "Weird, it must have rained."

"We have to slow down or we're going to wipe out."

The girls moved carefully down the wet trail. They tried focusing on the ground, but it was difficult. The charms were a constant reminder that their sister was in trouble.

"Em, *can* they combine

when we're not near Clare's pink charm?"

"No idea," Emmy replied. "And what happens if Clare's the one we need to save? Will the magic still work?"

"I think we're about to find out. Come on!"

Meanwhile, inside the enclosure, Clare waited, listening for Fluffy's bark, when she felt a gentle pull on her ear. She reached up to touch her charm, which lifted toward the blocked entrance. *My charm! It's activating. Are Emmy and Giselle close by?* Then she heard a beautiful sound from the other side of the rock.

"Clare!" called Giselle.

"Trills, in here!"

"Are you okay?"

Clare felt a sharp stab of guilt. Emmy

sounded so concerned. Why had she been so unkind to her sisters?

"I'm trapped," Clare cried. "There's a rock jamming the entranceway!"

"How did Fluffy get out?" asked Giselle.

Clare explained how the pup had clawed his way up a tree, then leapt to the top of the wall. "I couldn't see what happened. Is he okay?"

Emmy was about to tell Clare the pup was injured, but Giselle put a hand over her mouth. "Let's not worry her more. We'll figure out how to help Fluffy once we rescue Clare."

They placed the pup in a sunny spot to rest and got to work.

CHAPTER 15

Giselle and Emmy ran along the outside of the enclosure, searching for a way in, when their blue and green charms popped out of their jewelry and whooshed toward the top of the wall.

"Giselle, look! I think the charms are trying to combine," Emmy called out.

"I sure hope so," said Giselle. "Then we'll be able to rescue Clare."

But then—*Ping! Ping!*—Emmy looked up and gasped. Her green charm had hit the rock wall near the top and was clinging to it like a magnet. A few feet away, Giselle's blue charm had done the same thing.

"What was that noise, Trills?" Clare called.

Then—*Ping!*—Clare's pink charm slipped out of her earring and flew up, sticking to the inside of the rock wall. "My charm's trying to combine with yours, but the wall's in the way."

Giselle's brow creased with worry. "What are we going to do?"

Clare sucked in a breath and started to sniffle. She was trying to be brave, but she'd reached her limit.

"Clare, no. Don't cry," said Emmy gently through the wall.

"Yeah, sis. We'll figure this out. Besides, the ground's wet enough already."

Clare giggled through her sobs. It felt good to have her sisters back. "I just want to hug you guys!"

"And you will," called Emmy. "Because together, we're unstoppable."

"*Aroo!*" Claw cried, wiggling her bottom.

Suddenly, Fluffy barked, "*Rrrr, rrr, rrr.*" The pup limped over to the wall and nosed at a spot with his snout.

"What is it boy? What'd you find?" Giselle bent toward the pup and saw a little hole in the rock she hadn't noticed before. As she studied the wall, she realized there were similar spots all over it. *Could I wedge my foot in here, a finger there?* The more she studied the wall, the more excited she became. It reminded her of her favorite spot in the tree house—their climbing wall. She jumped up and fist-pumped the air. "Yaaasss! Trills, we can do this!"

"I love your enthusiasm," Clare replied, "but what exactly can we do?"

Giselle grinned. "We can climb this wall! There are handholds and footholds, like at home."

Clare leaned in. "Hmmm. I see what you mean. I think I can wiggle my

foot in here." She pushed the tip of her sneaker into a tight spot, and it held.

Giselle let out a whoop. "Last one to the top is a rotten flower!"

CHAPTER 16

"Remember, it's just like our wall at home," Giselle coached. "Put one hand up, followed by a foot, then repeat on the other side."

"Whoops!" Clare cried.

"What happened?" Emmy called. "You okay?"

"Yeah, the rock's slippery because it's wet."

"Cool," Giselle replied. "Just take it slowly."

"Whoa!" Emmy's foot slipped, but Giselle

put out a foot to steady her. "Thanks, sis. That was a close one."

The girls worked steadily, inching their way up the wall. Finally, Giselle neared her blue charm. She clung to the wall with one hand and pushed the charm free with the other. *Pop!* Her charm flew up and hovered in the air, like it was waiting for the others.

"My turn," said Emmy. She stretched as

far as she could and nudged her green charm with her fingertips until—*Wup!*—it sprang into the air and joined Giselle's blue charm above the wall.

"How you doing, Clare?" Giselle called.

"Not. Great." Clare grunted from the other side of the rock. "My charm won't budge."

"The powers from our charms may not have activated, but we're still sisters with brain power," Emmy said. "Let's use our heads. We'll figure this out."

"Wait. That's it!" Clare exclaimed. "Em, you're a genius."

"I am?"

"Oh, totally." Giselle smiled.

Clare inched her way farther up the wall, and then softly nudged her charm with the top of her head. The pink charm leapt toward the others, which were already hovering in the sky. And—*Zoom!*—the charms shot together, creating one beautiful, seamless trillium flower charm that glowed from within. As the newly formed charm floated down, Emmy snatched it from the air and tucked it into the pouch she wore around her waist.

In the next instant—*Whoosh!*—the mini'mals became full-size animals. With a final *fwomp*, the entire forest shimmered, and the girls were transformed. Though the sisters remained on opposite sides of the rock wall, in their warrior wear, they looked united, strong, and unstoppable.

"We did it! We are sisters with powers!" they cried.

Claw put her paws against the wall and tapped her nails against the stone. Clare could feel the vibration from the other side. "Aww, thanks, Claw. I can't wait to see you, too."

"I'm coming for ya, sis," Giselle called.

"I want to come," said Emmy. "I need to see with my own eyes that Clare is okay."

"No problem," said Giselle. Now super strong, she easily moved to where Emmy clung to the wall. "Get on my back, Em. I'll carry you safely to the top."

Giselle quickly scaled the wall. "I love a good climb. Especially when I've got power!"

She and Emmy rested on the ledge for a moment, peering down at their sister. "Clare looks okay," said Emmy. "Thank goodness."

Giselle smiled, swung her legs over the ledge, and picked her way down the interior wall to Clare. Meanwhile, Emmy carefully climbed back down the exterior where the now maxi-size pets were waiting.

Giselle jumped to the ground and Clare ran to her and hugged her tight. "Thank you for coming."

"We're sisters. Was there ever any doubt?"

"I was so mean to you guys," Clare began.

"Let's talk about that later. Right now, we have to reunite the team!" Giselle easily pulled

Clare onto her back and made her way up and over the rock wall. When they finally landed on the ground outside the enclosure, the girls held each other in a terrifically tight triplet hug. Then, they sank into the grass to catch their breath.

CHAPTER 17

Clare had only rested for a moment when and noticed Fluffy laying on his side. Clare jumped up. "Fluffy! Come here, boy."

Fluffy tried to stand, but the minute he put weight on his front leg, he whimpered and sank back to the ground.

"Guys, something's wrong with Fluffy," Clare called out as she ran to his side. "Poor boy! Did you get hurt when we powered up?

Emmy, could shooting up to maxi'mal size have done something to his leg?"

Emmy glanced at Giselle. In the rush to save Clare, they hadn't told her about Fluffy's injury. She put an arm around her sister's shoulders. "No, Fluffy hurt his leg when he was still mini. I think he sprained it when he went over the wall to get help."

"Oh, Fluff," cried Clare. She stroked his back and kissed his head.

Emmy looked around. "Hmmm. Maybe we can find something to make a splint?"

"Em," said Giselle. "What about your powers? They haven't let us down yet."

Emmy looked at her hands. She'd been so focused on rescuing Clare, she'd forgotten that she was able to close cuts and revive trampled plants simply by touching them. But she couldn't see Fluffy's injury the way she could spot a cut or a broken stem. Would her magic work when she couldn't touch the injury directly? After a deep breath, she met her sisters' eyes. "I can try."

Fluffy winced when Emmy put her hand out and ran

her finger lightly over the sore leg, top to bottom, barely touching it. She waited, but nothing happened. The mighty wolf whimpered and closed his eyes.

A few moments later, Fluffy raised his head. He wagged his tail, then carefully placed his paw on the ground, testing if he could put weight on it. Finally, he sprang to his feet and licked Emmy all over.

Claw and Soar raced to his side. Their calls rang through the forest. They sounded as happy as the sisters felt.

"Thank you, Emmy," Clare said, wrapping her arms around her wolf's neck. "Not only did you rescue me, you healed Fluffy."

"No need to thank me," Emmy replied.

Giselle put an arm around each of them.

"We're sisters. It's what we do."

"Trills, one more thing. I-I'm sorry." Clare's voice got wobbly. "I really wanted the show—"

"To be perfect," Giselle finished. "We know."

"Yes, but I never told you *why.*"

"Wasn't it so we could open the spa?" Emmy asked.

"Yes, but it was more than that." Clare took a deep breath. "I wanted everything to be perfect to prove I had a special way to help people the way you both do."

Giselle looked confused.

"What do you mean?" asked Emmy.

"G, you're always coaching Zee. He looks up to you. And Em, you take care of the animals at the clinic. Dad relies on you so much. But I didn't have a special way to help.

I thought if I could make everyone in Trillville feel good with the spa, I'd be more like the two of you."

"Oh, Clare," Emmy said, "you *are* special. You help *us* all the time!"

"I do?"

Giselle nodded. "You helped me with my outfit so I could have fun in the spring."

"And when you put my hair up, it made me feel cool," Emmy added. "I want to wear it that way all the time."

Clare smiled at her sisters and blinked back a few tears.

"And now," continued Emmy, "we're going to help you by saving this fashion show."

Clare hugged her sisters again. She would have stayed that way, but her gaze fell on the rock still jamming the entrance to the spring. "Trills, what are we going to do about that boulder? The show is supposed to start soon, but nobody is going to be able to get in!"

CHAPTER 18

Giselle walked over to the boulder stuck in the opening. "Allow me," she said. She braced her shoulder against it and pushed hard. "Huh?" she said, stepping back. "Even my super strength isn't enough to move this hunk of granite!"

"Whaddya say we get a bird's-eye view of the problem?" Emmy asked. She motioned to the hill opposite the enclosure. "I think I may have an idea."

"Bull's-eye to your bird's-eye," agreed Giselle.

The triplets linked arms and marched up the hill with the maxi'mals close behind.

At the top were rocks of all sizes and shapes. Some were even piled one on top of another.

"Hey, Trills, what do you think about going bowling?" asked Emmy.

"This doesn't seem like a good time for games," Clare replied. "Everyone's coming for a fashion show at sunset."

Giselle laughed. "I get it. If we can roll one of these boulders down the hill, maybe it can knock the rock blocking the entrance out of the way."

"I guess I'm not the only one in this family with great ideas," Clare said, genuinely impressed.

Giselle pushed her shoulder into one of the large rocks. "Ugh. It won't budge."

"Well, if there's one thing I've learned today, it's that there's nothing wrong with a little help," Clare said. "In fact, asking for help makes you stronger!" She aimed her super vision at the hillside. "There! On the other side of that tree is a big branch. Maybe we can use that to get this rock rolling."

Giselle raced over and returned with the branch. "Here goes nothing." She rammed the branch into the stone. The rock still wouldn't budge. "Now what?"

"Whatever we do, we'd better do it quickly," said Clare, looking up at the sky.

And that reminded Emmy to check the charm. The sisters' magic only lasted so long. "Oh no. Our trillium flower charm is fading. We really do have to hurry."

"Okay, I have another idea," Clare said. "It's a long shot, though. What if we all help?" She looked at her sisters and the maxi'mals.

"I love that you're thinking like a team again," said Emmy gently, "but Giselle has super strength, and if she can't move it, I'm not sure us pushing will make any difference."

"I'm not suggesting we all push," Clare explained. "I think we should all jump!"

"Huh?" Emmy and Giselle looked at Clare as though she had two heads.

"No time to explain, Trills. Just trust me."

"We do, sis," Emmy assured her.

"Okay, Claw, dig a hole under the rock." Clare pointed to exactly where she wanted it.

"*Grrh-huh*," Claw replied, scooping out the earth with her razor-sharp claws.

"Now, Giselle," Clare said, "slide one end of that branch into the hole and balance the middle of the branch on this smaller rock."

Giselle moved things into place.

"This reminds me of a seesaw," said Emmy.

"Exactly!" cried Clare. "We'll jump onto this side of the branch, and our weight will drive the other end of the branch up."

"And the force will launch the rock?" Giselle asked.

"Hopefully," said Clare.

Giselle smiled. "Seesawing and bowling! Can this day get any better?"

CHAPTER 19

"Ready?" called Emmy as they all prepared to jump.

"Set," Clare added.

"Bowwllll!" shouted Giselle. They jumped as high as they could, landing on the end of the branch together.

"AHHHH!!!" they screamed as they forced the branch to the ground. Like a seesaw, the other end lifted, raising the heavy rock up just enough to set it in motion.

Clare giggled. "Rock 'n' roll." The spinning rock picked up speed. Finally, it hit the boulder stuck in the entranceway. *Smack!* The impact was just enough to make the boulder roll to the side, clearing the opening to the enclosure.

"Stttt-rike!" Giselle cried.

"Best game of bowling ever!" Emmy declared.

The Trills and maxi'mals raced down the hill, through the now-clear entrance. "Yes! The boulder is out," Clare cheered. "Which means the fashion show is on!"

Their problem was fixed not a second too soon. *Poof!* The three petal charms separated.

Poof! The maxi'mals shrank to mini size.

Pfft! Emmy, Clare, and Giselle were once again in their normal clothes.

"Time's up," said Giselle.

"It doesn't matter," Clare said. "I don't need any magic with my sisters by my side."

With just a few hours until showtime, everyone got to work. Claw and Fluffy dragged the blankets, still damp from the rain, into the sunniest part of the enclosure where Soar fanned them with her wings to speed up the drying. Giselle grabbed the skimmer and cleared the leaves that had fallen during the storm from the pool while Emmy cleaned the cups and made sure *all* the umbrellas were leaning to the right.

Clare stood with her back to everyone in a far corner of the enclosure.

"What'cha doing over there, Clare?" Giselle asked.

"It's a surprise, but you're gonna love it."

When they'd finished, everything looked beautiful.

"Thanks, Trills," Clare said. "I couldn't have done this without the power of three."

With that, the girls scooped up their mini pets and ran home to get model-ready.

CHAPTER 20

As the sun set, the guests arrived and settled on the blankets, sipping daisy juice and admiring the decor. Fireflies lit the lanterns, creating a beautiful glow in the dusk.

Emmy nudged Giselle. They couldn't believe their eyes. People were snacking on jelly beans, and the colors were mixed!

"I knew they would like a rainbow!" Giselle said. "Who mixed them up?"

"Me!" said Clare. "The jelly beans look better together, just like we do!" As the girls hugged, their blond, brown, and auburn hair mixed just like the candy.

Soon, the fireflies dimmed. The show was about to start.

"We'd wish you good luck, but you don't need it," Emmy said.

"Yeah, you've got this," added Giselle.

"Thanks, you guys," Clare squeezed her sisters' hands. "I just have one more idea to make this show perfect."

"Spill, Trill," said Emmy.

"You two should walk in the show with me."

Giselle and Emmy jumped up.

"Is that a yes?" Clare asked with a laugh.

"Abso-trilly," Giselle responded.

The music started, and Dr. J.A. strolled onto the runway. He wore the turquoise loafers along with orange and turquoise shorts and a bright white shirt with turquoise trim.

Giselle's and Emmy's mouths dropped open. Dad didn't own anything nearly that cool. But Clare was the most surprised. Where had he found an outfit to match those shoes? She giggled. "I guess everyone in our family knows how to make things happen!"

Next up was Mrs. Lilienstern, wearing a beautiful dress. The top was sky blue and the bottom was a sequined multi-tiered skirt in all different shades from turquoise to navy.

The crowd cheered.

Then Mayor Mae strutted down the runway. Her geode necklace was framed by her powder-blue silk tank dress. The stone shimmered in the evening light.

Finally, it was the sisters' turn.

"Ready, Trills?" Clare asked, as she took her sisters' hands. The mini'mals stood next to them, each wearing a custom blue collar. Fluffy looked particularly proud of his outfit.

"Where did those collars come from?" asked Giselle.

"They are too cute," squealed Emmy.

"I told you you'd love the surprise." Clare grinned. "And I have one more." She dipped her hand into a bag and placed the bejeweled cat headbands from Mrs. Lilienstern's shop on their heads. "*Purr*fect. Let's go, team!"

As the triplets made their way down the runway, the guests stood and cheered.

Emmy turned to Clare. "Take a bow."

"Yeah, C. Nobody worked harder than you to make this all happen."

Giselle and Emmy stood aside to let their sister enjoy the applause. Clare smiled from ear to ear.

After the last guest had gone, the sisters counted the money they'd raised.

"Looks like we have more than enough for spa supplies!" Emmy announced.

"I can't wait to get them," Clare said with a yawn. "For now, though, who's ready to go home? It's been a long day."

Dr. J.A. and Zee were waiting for them right outside the enclosure.

"Dad, you looked incredible!" Clare said. "I can't believe you put together that outfit."

"I learned from the best," he replied.

"Zee, you helped with Dad's outfit?" Clare asked.

"Yup. I learned from the best." He threw his arms around Clare's waist, and together, the family headed home.

CHAPTER 21

"Ready to shop?" Clare asked the next morning, tucking the money they'd made from the fashion show into her purse.

"Ready!" Giselle and Emmy replied.

At the store, Clare turned to Giselle and Emmy. "We should use whatever colors you like best for the spa, not just my favorites."

"Yeah," Giselle teased. "Besides, sparkly colors are soooo last season."

"Bull's-eye." Clare giggled.

The sisters filled their baskets with everything they'd need: lots of polishes, towels, lotions, nail files, and cucumbers.

Back at the spring, Giselle and Emmy started to unpack the supplies.

"What ya got there, G?" Emmy asked when Giselle reached into her pocket for the fourth time.

"I can't help myself. They're so good." She uncurled her fingers and held out a handful of jelly beans. "Hey, Clare, can we serve these at the spa?"

"Great idea, sis," Clare replied. She held up a banner. "Come on, Trills. I can't put this up without your help."

Together, they unfurled and hung the

banner. It read: WELCOME TO THE SISTERS'
SOAK AND SPRING.

"Yoo-hoo!" Mrs. Lilienstern called. She
rushed over, clutching a bottle of nail polish.
Behind her, the Trills could see a line
forming. They ran to their places.

Clare sat down to check in the guests.
The mini'mals stood nearby, eager to be
relax'imals for any guest who wanted to pet
a cuddly friend while they soaked in the
pool. Emmy was in charge of the nail polish
area. Giselle snuck one last jelly bean before
grabbing a pile of fluffy towels.

The sisters were ready to do what they did
best—work together. When they did that,
they were truly unstoppable.

Laura Brown is an early childhood expert and has served as Content Expert and Research Director for Nick Jr., Disney Junior, Amazon Kids, DreamWorks Animation Television, PBS Kids, Universal Kids, and many others. She lives in Tenafly, New Jersey.

Elly Kramer is currently the VP of Production & Development at Imagine Entertainment in their Kids and Family division. She has created and led the development of numerous award-winning TV shows, online games, and apps, and has produced and developed over thirty-five shorts. She lives in Los Angeles, California.